Colin Kaepernick

FOOTBALL STARS UP CLOSE
★ ★ ★

by Nel Yomtov

Consultant: Barry Wilner
AP Football Writer

BEARPORT
PUBLISHING

New York, New York

Credits

Cover and Title Page, © Tony Avelar/AP Images; 4, © Robbins Photography; 5, © Kevin Terrell/AP Images; 6, © Ben Liebenberg/AP Images; 7, © Hector Amezcua/AP Images; 8, © Yearbook Library; 9, © Cathleen Allison/AP Images; 10, © Yearbook Library; 11, © Debbie Noda/AP Images; 12, © Marcio Jose Sanchez/AP Images; 13, © Matt York/AP Images; 14, © Matt Cilley/AP Images; 15, © Michael Conroy/AP Images; 16, © Robbins Photography; 17, © Robbins Photography; 18, © Dave Martin/AP Images; 19, © Dave Martin/AP Images; 20, © Tom Hauck/AP Images; 21, © Gerald Herbert/AP Images; 22, © Robbins Photography.

Publisher: Kenn Goin
Editor: Jessica Rudolph
Creative Director: Spencer Brinker
Photo Researcher: Josh Gregory
Design: Emily Love

Library of Congress Cataloging-in-Publication Data

Yomtov, Nelson.
  Colin Kaepernick / by Nel Yomtov.
      pages cm. — (Football stars up close)
  Includes bibliographical references and index.
  ISBN 978-1-62724-085-7 (library binding) — ISBN 1-62724-085-3 (library binding)
 1. Kaepernick, Colin, 1987—Juvenile literature. 2. Football players—United States—Biography—Juvenile literature. I. Title.
  GV939.K25Y65 2014
  796.332092—dc23
  [B]
                                                    2013037787

For more information, write to Bearport Publishing Company, Inc., 45 West 21st Street, Suite 3B, New York, New York 10010. Printed in the United States of America.

10 9 8 7 6 5 4 3 2 1

Contents

The Big Play

It was January 12, 2013. The San Francisco 49ers were going head-to-head against the Green Bay Packers in the **NFL playoffs**. The game was tied 24–24 in the third quarter. Colin Kaepernick, the 49ers' **quarterback**, took the **snap**. Instead of passing, however, he gripped the ball and charged down the field. A race to the **end zone** was on!

Colin wears #7 for the San Francisco 49ers. The team's nickname is the "Niners."

Colin stands six feet four inches tall (1.9 m) and weighs 230 pounds (104 kg). However, his big size doesn't keep him from being one of the fastest quarterbacks in the NFL.

One Step Closer

Several Packers tried to tackle Colin, but he was too fast. In a few seconds, he ran 56 yards (51 m) to score a **touchdown**! By the time the game was over, the 49ers had scored two more touchdowns. They beat the Packers 45–31. Colin and the 49ers were one step closer to playing in the **Super Bowl**!

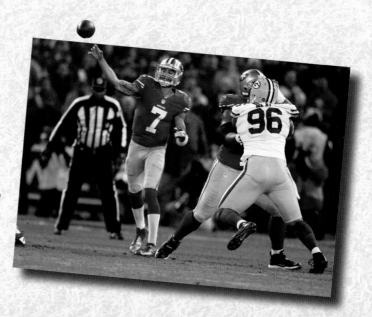

Colin threw for 263 yards (240.5 m) and two touchdowns against the Packers.

In the 2012–2013 season, Colin scored five touchdowns by running the ball into the end zone himself.

In the game against the Packers, Colin ran for 181 yards (165.5 m), setting an NFL single-game playoff record for most rushing yards by a quarterback.

Hopes and Dreams

Colin Rand Kaepernick was born in Milwaukee, Wisconsin, on November 3, 1987. His family moved to California four years later. As a child, Colin's speed and strength made him good at many sports. In the fourth grade, he wrote a letter to himself about his dream to play in the NFL. Colin worked hard to make his dream come true. At age nine, he was already his youth team's **starting** quarterback.

Colin as a baby

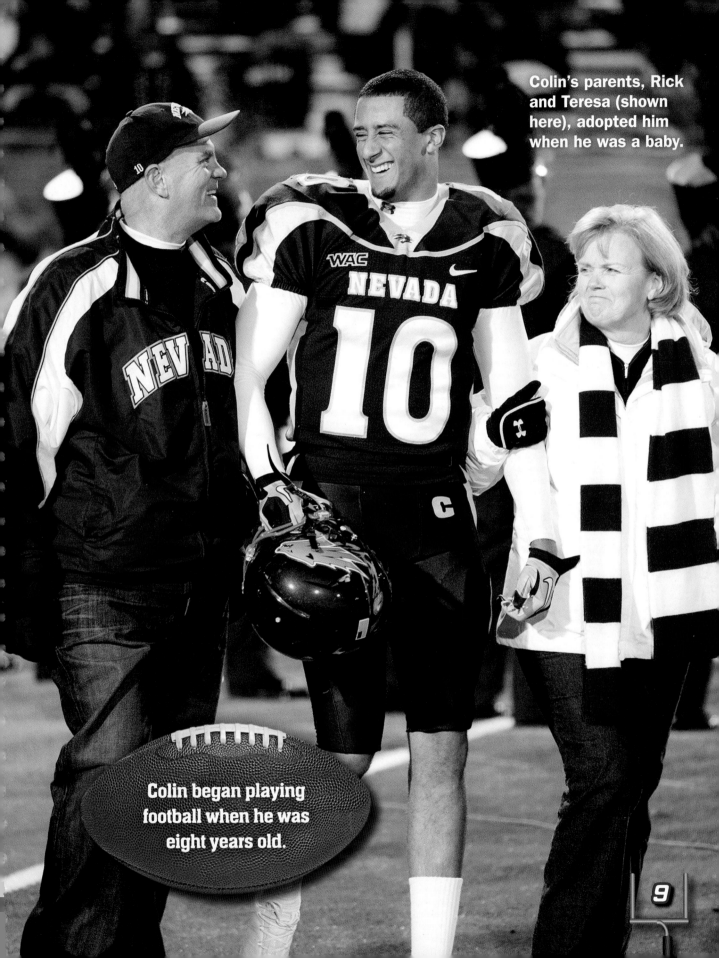

Colin's parents, Rick and Teresa (shown here), adopted him when he was a baby.

Colin began playing football when he was eight years old.

Two-Sport Superstar

In high school, Colin played football and baseball. His powerful arm helped him be a terrific quarterback and a great **pitcher**. In his senior year, Colin led his football team to its first-ever playoff victory. That same year, his incredibly fast pitches led him to an amazing 11–2 record on the baseball field. He struck out player after player with his fastballs. Colleges began to take notice of Colin's unbelievable skills.

Colin playing football for John H. Pitman High School in Turlock, California

Tradition Maker,
Coach
Brandon Harris,
Bulldog Slayer

In high school, Colin could throw a baseball **92** miles per hour (148 kph)!

At John H. Pitman High School, Brandon Harris (right) coached Colin's football team, the Pride.

Football or Baseball?

Many colleges offered Colin a baseball **scholarship**, but he turned them down. His dream was to play football. Luckily, the coaches at the University of Nevada, Reno, were wowed by Colin's strong arm and speed. They offered Colin a football scholarship—the only offer he got. Colin jumped at the chance!

Colin (left) bonded quickly with the other players on the University of Nevada football team, known as the Wolf Pack.

Colin (left) was thrilled to earn a football scholarship from the University of Nevada.

Many colleges did not offer Colin a football scholarship because they thought he was too skinny and might get injured easily.

One of the Best

In his first season at Nevada, Colin started out as the **backup** quarterback. During the fifth game, however, the starting quarterback was injured. Colin stepped in. Fans cheered as he passed for 384 yards (351 m) and scored four touchdowns. Colin played so well that he became the team's new starting quarterback. By graduation, Colin was one of the best football players in the country. He now had his eye on the NFL **draft**.

Colin (right) leaps for a touchdown in a 2007 college game against Boise State.

Colin (#10) threw 21 touchdown passes during his senior year at Nevada.

In the 2008–2009 season, Colin became only the fifth player in college football history to pass for at least 2,000 yards (1,829 m) and rush for at least 1,000 yards (914 m) in one season.

A Dream Come True

In 2011, Colin's childhood dream came true when the San Francisco 49ers drafted him. In his **rookie** season, he was the backup to quarterback Alex Smith. The following season, Alex got hurt in a game. Colin made his first NFL start in the next game, on November 19, 2012, against the Chicago Bears. Colin helped crush the Bears 32–7! Eventually, Alex got better, but Colin was on fire. The Niners' coach kept Colin as the starting quarterback. Best of all, Colin led his team to the playoffs!

Colin didn't play much during his rookie season in the NFL.

Colin passed for 1,814 yards (1,659 m) during the 2012–2013 season.

The Niners finished the 2012–2013 season with 11 wins, 4 losses, and a tie.

Playoff Action

In the first game of the playoffs, the 49ers defeated the Packers. In the next round, the Niners took on the Atlanta Falcons. At halftime, the Falcons led 24–14. Things looked bad, but Colin wouldn't give up. He and the 49ers launched a **comeback** that led to a 28–24 victory. In his first year as starting quarterback, Colin guided his team to the Super Bowl!

In the playoff game against the Atlanta Falcons, Colin passed for 233 yards (213 m) and one touchdown.

The 49ers' victory over the Falcons was one of the biggest comebacks in NFL playoff history.

The 2012–2013 season marked the Niners' first Super Bowl appearance in 18 years.

Super Bowl Face-Off

At the Super Bowl, the 49ers had a tough time against the Baltimore Ravens. The Niners were behind 21–6 at halftime. Colin's accurate passing helped narrow the gap, though. With four minutes left, they were behind only 34–29. Yet there wasn't enough time to win. The 49ers lost 34–31, but today Colin still has the attitude of a winner. "I just try to keep my head down, keep working, and not worry about anything else," he says. Colin's incredible story is just beginning.

Super Bowl XLVII (47) was played in New Orleans, Louisiana, on February 3, 2013.

Colin (left) throwing a pass during the Super Bowl

More than 108 million people watched on television as Colin and the 49ers faced off against the Ravens in the Super Bowl.

Colin's Life and Career

★ **November 3, 1987** Colin Kaepernick is born in Milwaukee, Wisconsin.

★ **1991** Colin moves to California with his family.

★ **1996** At age nine, Colin becomes the starting quarterback on his youth football team.

★ **2002–2006** Colin plays football and baseball for Pitman High School in Turlock, California.

★ **2006** Colin accepts a football scholarship to attend the University of Nevada.

★ **2008** Colin totals 3,979 yards (3,638 m) and 39 touchdowns in his sophomore year at the University of Nevada.

★ **2011** Colin is drafted by the San Francisco 49ers.

★ **2012** Colin plays his first NFL game as a starter and helps beat the Chicago Bears 32–7.

★ **2013** Colin sets an NFL single-game playoff record for most rushing yards by a quarterback, with 181 yards (165.5 m).

★ **2013** Colin plays in his first Super Bowl.

Glossary

backup (BAK-uhp) a player who doesn't play at the start of a game and often doesn't play at all; the second-best player in a position

comeback (KUHM-bak) a situation in which a team that is losing quickly scores enough points to close the gap

draft (DRAFT) an event in which professional football teams take turns choosing college athletes to play for them

end zone (END ZOHN) the area at either end of a football field where touchdowns are scored

NFL (EN-EFF-ELL) letters standing for the National Football League, which includes 32 teams

pitcher (PICH-ur) the baseball player who throws the ball to the batter

playoffs (PLAY-awfss) the games held after the end of the regular football season that determine which two teams will compete in the Super Bowl

quarterback (KWOR-tur-bak) a football player who leads the offense, the part of a team that moves the ball forward

rookie (RUK-ee) a person in his or her first season in a sport

scholarship (SKOL-ur-ship) money given to a person so that he or she can go to college

snap (SNAP) the action in which a football is handed to the quarterback, beginning a play

starting (START-ing) being the coach's first choice to play in a game

Super Bowl (SOO-pur BOHL) the final championship game of the NFL season

touchdown (TUHCH-doun) a score of six points that is made by getting the football across the other team's goal line

Index

Bibliography

Official Site of the NFL: www.nfl.com

Official Site of the San Francisco 49ers: www.49ers.com

Sessler, Marc. "Colin Kaepernick Foretold Future in Fourth-Grade Letter." www.nfl.com (December 17, 2012).

Read More

Hoblin, Paul. *Colin Kaepernick: NFL Phenom (Playmakers)*. Minneapolis, MN: ABDO (2014).

Stewart, Mark. *The San Francisco 49ers (Team Spirit)*. Chicago: Norwood House (2013).

Whiting, Jim. *The Story of the San Francisco 49ers (NFL Today)*. Mankato, MN: Creative Education (2014).

Learn More Online

To learn more about Colin Kaepernick, visit
www.bearportpublishing.com/FootballStarsUpClose